A PIG, A FOX, AND A FOX

For teachers, past and present,
with gratefulness and admiration—JF

PENGUIN WORKSHOP
An Imprint of Penguin Random House LLC, New York

Penguin supports copyright. Copyright fuels creativity, encourages diverse voices, promotes free speech, and creates a vibrant culture. Thank you for buying an authorized edition of this book and for complying with copyright laws by not reproducing, scanning, or distributing any part of it in any form without permission. You are supporting writers and allowing Penguin to continue to publish books for every reader.

Copyright © 2020 by Jonathan Fenske. All rights reserved. Published by Penguin Workshop, an imprint of Penguin Random House LLC, New York. PENGUIN and PENGUIN WORKSHOP are trademarks of Penguin Books Ltd, and the W colophon is a registered trademark of Penguin Random House LLC. Manufactured in China.

Visit us online at www.penguinrandomhouse.com.

Library of Congress Cataloging-in-Publication Data is available.

ISBN 9781524792121 (paperback)   10 9 8 7 6 5 4 3 2 1
ISBN 9780593382561 (library binding)   10 9 8 7 6 5 4 3 2 1

A PIG, A FOX, AND A FOX

by Jonathan Fenske

Penguin Workshop

PART ONE

5

I look around.
Where is that Fox?

Tee-hee.

I see a wall.
A wall of blocks.

11

I see Fox sitting on the wall!

If those blocks tip, that Fox will fall!

I bumped the wall.
The wall of blocks.

The wall will fall!
And so will Fox!

I will catch you!
Do not fear!

Your good friend Pig
is always here!

15

PLOP!

16

18

PART TWO

23

That sneaky Fox.
He is so bad!

That sneaky Fox.
He makes me mad!

26

But we have had enough today.